The SUMMER OLYMPICS

ON THE WORLD STAGE

GREATEST MOMENTS

The
SUMMER OLYMPICS
ON THE WORLD STAGE

ATHLETES TO WATCH
FASCINATING FACTS
GREATEST MOMENTS
RECORD BREAKERS

The SUMMER OLYMPICS
ON THE WORLD STAGE

GREATEST MOMENTS

GREG BACH

MC

MASON CREST
PHILADELPHIA | MIAMI

MASON CREST
450 Parkway Drive, Suite D, Broomall, Pennsylvania 19008
(866) MCP-BOOK (toll-free) • www.masoncrest.com

First printing

9 8 7 6 5 4 3 2 1
ISBN (hardback) 978-1-4222-4446-3
ISBN (series) 978-1-4222-4443-2
ISBN (ebook) 978-1-4222-7367-8

Library of Congress Cataloging-in-Publication Data

Names: Bach, Greg, author.
Title: Greatest moments / Greg Bach.
Description: Broomall, PA : Mason Crest, 2020. | Series: The Summer Olympics : on the world stage | Includes bibliographical references and index.
Identifiers: LCCN 2019038973 | ISBN 9781422244463 (hardback) | ISBN 9781422273678 (ebook)
Subjects: LCSH: Olympics–History–Juvenile literature.
Classification: LCC GV721.53 .B34 2020 | DDC 796.48–dc23
LC record available at https://lccn.loc.gov/2019038973

Developed and Produced by National Highlights Inc.
Editor: Andrew Luke
Production: Crafted Content LLC

Cover images, clockwise from top left:

American track star Jessie Owens (Bundesarchiv, Bild 183-R96374@Wikimedia Commons), Members of Team USA during the 2008 Summer Olympics opening ceremony (Tim Hipps, U.S. Army@public domain), American track star Carl Lewis (KUHT@ Wikimedia Commons), German weightlifter Matthias Steiner (Dacoucou@Wikimedia Commons)

QR CODES AND LINKS TO THIRD-PARTY CONTENT

CONTENTS

WHAT ARE THE SUMMER OLYMPICS?

The ancient Olympic Games took place in Greece every four years for nearly 12 centuries from 776 BC through 393 AD. They were part of a religious festival to honor Zeus, who was the father of Greek gods and goddesses. The event was held in Olympia, a sanctuary site named for Mount Olympus, which is the country's tallest mountain and the mythological home of the Greek gods. It is the place for which the Olympics are named.

Roughly 1,500 years after the ancient Games ended, a Frenchman named Baron Pierre de Coubertin wanted to resurrect the Olympic Games to coincide with the 1900 World Fair in Paris. The 1900 Paris Exposition was to feature the newest, modern-day, turn-of-the-century attractions like talking films, the diesel engine, escalators, magnet audio recorders, and a fairly new Eiffel Tower painted yellow.

De Coubertin wanted the best athletes in the world for the first modern Olympic Games outside of Greece, so he presented the idea in 1894. Representatives from 34 potential countries got so excited about his plan that they proposed the Games take place in 1896 instead. So, the modern Olympics, as it is now called, began where the ancient Games left off—in Athens, Greece, in 1896.

The 10-day event in April 1896 had 241 male athletes from 14 countries competing in 43 events. The events at these Athens Games were athletics (track and field), swimming, cycling, fencing, gymnastics, shooting, tennis, weightlifting, and wrestling. The ancient Games had consisted of short races, days-long boxing matches, and chariot races.

Like the ancient Games, organizers held the event every four years, with Paris hosting in 1900, when women made their first appearance. The Paris Games had many more competitors, as 997 athletes represented 24 countries in 95 total events. These Games were spread out from May through October to coincide with the Paris Exposition.

The Summer Olympics have now spanned into the 21st century and have become the ultimate crowning achievement for athletes worldwide. The Games have evolved with the addition and removal of events, the scope of media coverage, the addition of a separate Winter Olympics, and the emergence of both the Special Olympics and Paralympic Games.

The Olympics have been the site of great athletic feats and sportsmanship. They have presented tragedy, triumph, controversy, and political grandstanding. There have been legendary athletes, remarkable human-interest stories, doping allegations, boycotts, terrorist attacks, and three cancellations because of worldwide war.

Yet the Olympics, with its five interlocking rings and eternal flame, remain a symbol of unity and hope.

The United States hosted its first Games in 1904 in St. Louis, Missouri, which, like Paris, spread the Games over several months in conjunction with the World Fair. The presentation of gold, silver, and bronze medals for finishing first, second, and third in each event began at this Olympics.

More than 2,000 athletes competed in England at the 1908 London Games, which were originally scheduled for Rome but reassigned once organizers discovered the Italian capital would not be ready in time. In London, the marathon race was extended by 195 meters so the finish line would be just below the royal box in the stadium and thus the 26.2 miles from the 1908 edition went on to become the official marathon distance beginning with the 1924 Paris Games.

Stockholm, Sweden, hosted the 1912 Games, and the Olympics were cancelled in 1916 because of World War I (WWI). Other years in which the Olympic Games were not held include 1940 and 1944 because of World War II.

Berlin, Germany, had been awarded the 1916 Olympics that were cancelled, but rather than reward the Germans following WWI by giving them the 1920 Games, they were instead awarded to Antwerp, Belgium, to honor the Belgians who suffered so many hardships during the war. The Olympic flag, which shows five interlocked rings to signify the universality of the Games, was first hoisted during the 1920 opening ceremonies in Antwerp. The Olympic rings have become a well-known symbol of sportsmanship and unity worldwide.

The 1924 Games were back in Paris, and the Olympics became a recognized, bona fide worldwide event. The number of participating countries went from 29 to 44. There were more than 3,000 athletes competing and more than 1,000 journalists covering the competition.

Also, in 1924, the annual event became known as the Summer Olympics, or Summer Games, as the Winter Olympics debuted in Chamonix, France. The Winter Games were held every four years through 1992. The Winter Olympics were then held again in 1994 and every four years since then.

Two more long-standing traditions began at the 1928 Summer Games in Amsterdam, Netherlands. The Olympic flame was lit for the first time in a cauldron at the top of the Olympic stadium. Also, during the opening ceremony, the national team of Greece entered the stadium first and the Dutch entered last, signifying the first team to host the modern Olympics and the current host. This tradition still stands today.

The United States got its second Summer Olympics in 1932, when Los Angeles, California, hosted. The city built a lavish coliseum for

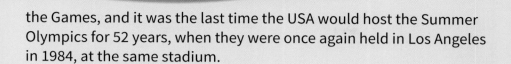

the Games, and it was the last time the USA would host the Summer Olympics for 52 years, when they were once again held in Los Angeles in 1984, at the same stadium.

The 1936 Summer Olympics in Berlin also produced some long-lasting, first-time traditions. These Games were the first to have a torch relay bringing the Olympic flame to the stadium, and they were also the first to be televised.

The Summer Olympics took a 12-year hiatus because of World War II, and London was once again called upon to host the Games with short notice in 1948.

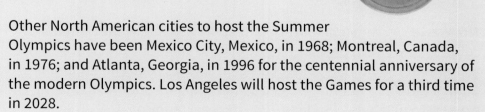

The Summer Games have been held every four years since 1948. In 2016, Rio de Janeiro, Brazil, hosted the Summer Games, and that meant the Olympics had now been held on five continents. Australia has hosted the Summer Olympics twice (Melbourne in 1956 and Sydney in 2000). Asia has hosted four times (Tokyo, Japan in 1964 and 2020; Seoul, Korea, in 1988; and Beijing, China, in 2008).

Other North American cities to host the Summer Olympics have been Mexico City, Mexico, in 1968; Montreal, Canada, in 1976; and Atlanta, Georgia, in 1996 for the centennial anniversary of the modern Olympics. Los Angeles will host the Games for a third time in 2028.

Although athletes typically garner headlines for most Olympic coverage, sometimes events outside of the playing field force the world to take notice.

Eight Palestinian terrorists shot two Israeli athletes dead and held nine more as hostages during the 1972 Munich Games in Germany. Those nine were also murdered during a botched rescue attempt.

The 1980 Moscow Games in Russia saw the fewest number of athletes in a Summer Olympics since 1956, when the USA led a boycott of Moscow after the Soviet Union invaded Afghanistan in December of 1979.

The Soviet Union then led a contingency of Eastern European nations that boycotted the 1984 Los Angeles Games during the Cold War, mainly as payback for the U.S. boycott.

The first Summer Olympics that were boycott-free since 1972 were the 1992 Games in Barcelona, Spain, which was also the first time professional basketball players competed, opening the door for professionals in all Olympic sports except wrestling and boxing. Before the International Olympic Committee (IOC) approved professional athletes to participate in the late 1980s, the Olympics were primarily for the world's best amateur athletes.

Many have lamented the demise of amateurism at the Olympic Games, but by far the most contentious issue the IOC has dealt with in recent years is the scourge of steroids and other prohibited performance-enhancing drugs.

The world's greatest celebration of sport has had a checkered and colorful past, from politics and doping to sheer athleticism and the triumph of the human spirit. This century has seen the Summer Games return to familiar places (Athens 2004, London 2012) and expand to new ones (Sydney 2000, Rio de Janeiro 2016). Tokyo awaits the world in 2020, when the newest great Olympic stories will be told.

– *Scott McDonald, Olympic and Paralympic Journalist*

GREATEST SUMMER OLYMPIC MOMENTS OF ALL TIME

The Summer Olympics have provided some of the most memorable moments in the history of sports. Gracing the calendar once every four years, amazing athletes from across the globe have gathered to compete on the world's grandest stage since the first Games of the modern era in 1896 in Athens, Greece, displaying spectacular athleticism, courage, and unbreakable spirit.

In *Greatest Moments*, part of the four-title *The Summer Olympics: On the World Stage* series, we introduce and take a closer look at the athletes and moments that showcase what the Summer Olympics are all about. There is American sprinter Jesse Owens, winner of four gold medals at the 1936 Games in Berlin under the gaze of a monstrous dictator; Michael Phelps, who won an impossible-to-believe eight gold medals at the 1988 Games in Seoul; and 14-year-old Romanian gymnast Nadia Comăneci, who famously scored seven perfect 10s in Montreal when no one had ever received even *one* perfect score in any Olympic competition before. There is also Bob Mathias, winner of the decathlon as a 17-year-old in 1948, still the youngest to ever do so; and dynamic gymnast Mary Lou Retton, who shot to fame at the 1984 Los Angeles Games by becoming the first American woman to win the all-around title.

The Games have been punctuated by plenty of history-rich moments too, reminding us of the true power of sports. There are North and South Korea, two countries that have been split for decades, but which walked into the opening ceremonies of the 2000 Sydney Games together under one flag; and the first-ever Refugee Olympic Team, featuring 10 unbelievably brave athletes who competed at the 2016 Rio de Janeiro Games.

Greatest Moments covers all these stories, plus Usain Bolt, Florence Griffith-Joyner, Mark Spitz, Michael Johnson, Cathy Freeman, Greg Louganis, and many more.

ERIC THE EEL
AFRICAN SWIMMER "WINS" HIS HEAT

Sydney 2000: Swimming

When Eric Moussambani from Equatorial Guinea arrived in Sydney after three days of travel to compete in the 100-meter freestyle at the 2000 Summer Olympics, there was a lot for the 22-year-old to take in. For starters, he had never been outside his small country in central Africa before. Then there was this—he had never been in an Olympic-size pool.

To help cultivate the Olympic spirit in developing nations, in the 1990s the IOC began allowing a handful of wild card entries to skip qualifying rounds and go directly to competing in the Olympics. So, on a Tuesday morning at the Sydney Olympic Park Aquatic Centre, Moussambani found himself on the starting blocks for the opening heat of the men's 100-meter freestyle with two other swimmers. As it happened, those two were soon disqualified for false starts, leaving him to swim the race alone.

Moussambani's training leading up to the Olympics had been limited to swimming in a 20-meter pool at a hotel in his hometown. When the starter's pistol fired, he dove into an Olympic-size pool to start a race for the first time in his life. The 17,000 spectators watched Moussambani struggling to complete the race, and began to cheer him on. They got louder and louder until he touched the wall in

GLOBAL ACCLAIM

When Moussambani exited the pool following his first 100-meter race he was thrust into the global spotlight. With an avalanche of interview requests, Olympic officials had to provide him with a personal assistant and a translator to handle it all. In the Olympic Village a banner reading "Eric the swimmer lives here" hung outside his room.

1:52.72 to "win" his heat. While that was the slowest time in Olympic history, and missed qualifying by more than 40 seconds, he became a beloved figure who embodied the Olympic spirit of doing your best.

"I couldn't feel my legs in the middle of the swimming pool. I was just moving and feeling that I am in the same place. But when I started hearing people calling, people shouting 'Go! Go! Go!', that gave me more strength and power to finish."
— Eric "The Eel" Moussambani

PASSPORT MISHAP

Moussambani dreamed of returning to the 2004 Summer Olympics in Athens, but his government's mishandling of his passport prevented him from making a second Olympic appearance.

SUPER SPITZ
AMERICAN WINS SEVEN GOLD MEDALS

Munich 1972: Swimming

A super-talented and mega-confident 18-year-old Mark Spitz had set 10 world records by the time the 1968 Summer Olympics rolled around, and he boldly predicted he would take home six gold medals from Mexico City. Instead, those Games didn't go as he envisioned. Spitz won just two gold medals, both in relay events, as well as a meager silver and bronze in individual events, falling far short of what he had talked about to the media.

Fast forward four years to Munich and the 1972 Summer Games, and a stronger, better (he was named World Swimmer of the Year in 1971), and quieter Spitz was more than ready. He had enjoyed a spectacular career at Indiana University, winning eight individual National Collegiate Athletic Association (NCAA) titles.

At Munich, Spitz let his swimming strokes do the talking for him— and he crushed the field. Seven races yielded seven gold medals. Spitz set a world record in every single one of them.

TERROR AND TRAGEDY

On September 5, less than 24 hours after Spitz's historic seventh gold medal, Palestinian terrorists attacked Israeli quarters in the Olympic Village, killing an Israeli coach and wrestler and taking nine other Israeli team members hostage, all of whom were later killed. Spitz, who is Jewish, was flown to London because some feared he might be a target.

Spitz won his sixth gold medal by edging out teammate Jerry Heidenreich in the 100-meter freestyle. This topped the previous record for a man of five gold medals at a single Olympic Games won by Italian fencer Nedo Nadi at the 1920 Games in Antwerp, Belgium. When Spitz secured his seventh gold medal, won as part of the 400-meter medley relay team, his U.S. teammates celebrated the moment by carrying him around the pool on their shoulders. Spitz is one of just five Olympians to win at least nine career gold medals.

36 YEAR STRETCH

Spitz held the record for most gold medals (seven) won at a single Olympic Games for 36 years, until Michael Phelps broke it by winning eight gold medals in 2008 at the Beijing Games.

LEAP OF THE CENTURY
BEAMON SETS UNTHINKABLE RECORD

Mexico City 1968: Long Jump

As Bob Beamon prepared to charge down the runway and launch himself into the Mexico City air for his first attempt in the 1968 Olympic long jump finals, no one could have imagined what would happen.

On his first jump the native of Queens, New York generated terrific speed on his approach and soared into the pit. As it turned out, Beamon had out-jumped the optical device that was installed to measure jumps, forcing officials to use tape measures to manually record what would soon become known as the Leap of the Century.

The long wait for the measurement to be taken led Beamon to think that perhaps he might have clipped the world record of 27 feet 4¾ inches by an inch or so. Well, he was partly right. Beamon did indeed have the world record, but he had completely crushed it. In a single leap he became the first to ever jump more than 28 feet *and* 29 feet. His jump of 29 feet 2½ inches (8.90 meters) bettered the world record by a mind-boggling 21.75 inches (55.2 centimeters). Some attributed the leap to the thin air in the high altitude of Mexico City, combined with the wind that

LENGTHY LEAP LASTS LONG TIME

Beamon's enormous world-record long jump was so good that day in Mexico City that it appeared untouchable—and for many years it held up as a mark that might never be broken. Beamon's record stood for nearly 23 years until Philadelphia's Mike Powell broke it—by almost 2 inches (5 centimeters)—at the 1991 World Championships in Tokyo.

was measured as the maximum allowed to be considered for a record jump. Beamon collapsed on the infield, overwhelmed with emotion as teammates and competitors alike surrounded to congratulate him.

No one else in the field came close to Beamon's epic leap, earning him worldwide praise for an amazing feat. Many have said it is the greatest achievement in Olympic history.

HOLDING STEADY

Beamon's leap of 8.9 meters is still the Olympic record and the second-longest wind-legal jump in history. The longest jump (and current world record) belongs to Philadelphia's Mike Powell. At the 1991 World Championships, Powell jumped an unprecedented 29 feet 4¼ inches (8.95 meters). Just as Beamon's did, Powell's world record has also stood for more than two decades.

A SURE THING
BOLT SMASHES TWO WORLD RECORDS

Beijing 2008: Track and Field

Entertaining and electrifying, Usain Bolt brought his megawatt smile and history-making speed to Beijing for the 2008 Summer Olympics and did what he always does on the world's grandest stage: win in big and convincing fashion and have a lot of fun in doing it.

In the 100-meter final, the Jamaican juggernaut accelerated past the fastest sprinters on the planet with ease. Bolt went into celebration mode with 20 meters left in the race, slapping his chest and easing up—and he still set a world record with a time of 9.69 seconds. This lowered the record of 9.72 seconds that Bolt had run a couple of months earlier at a meet in New York. It also broke Donovan Bailey's Olympic record of 9.84 set back in 1996 at the Atlanta Games. Richard Thompson (9.89) of Trinidad and Tobago and Walter Dixon (9.91) of the United States both ran personal bests for silver and bronze, respectively.

It was a different distance but the same story in the 200-meter final. Bolt outclassed a great field, running a 19.30 to break the great Michael Johnson's long-standing world record of 19.32

posted a dozen years earlier. Bolt was so dominant that he won by the largest margin of victory ever in a 200-meter Olympic final. Shawn Crawford (19.96) of the United States was next closest, taking silver.

When it came to the Olympics, Bolt was as good as anyone in the big moments: over three different Olympic Games, no competitor ever crossed the finish line before him in an Olympic final.

TEAMMATE DISGRACE

Bolt was a member of the Jamaican 4x100-meter relay team that won gold with a world-record performance in Beijing, only later to have their medals taken away when Nesta Carter was found to have taken a banned substance.

Usain Bolt set world records in both the 100 and 200 meters at the 2008 Olympics in Beijing.

STING LIKE A BEE
CLAY DOMINATES THE FIELD

Rome 1960: Boxing

When Cassius Clay arrived in Rome for the 1960 Summer Olympics, he quickly exhibited signs of the charisma and lethal boxing skills that would later make him a sports icon as Muhammad Ali, arguably the most loved, greatest, and most influential athlete the world has ever seen.

The light heavyweight from Louisville picked up the nickname of "The Mayor of the Olympic Village" in Rome because he was continually walking the premises, meeting athletes, and shaking hands. But when it came time to step into the ring, he was all business.

Clay won his first fight against Belgian Yvon Becaus when the referee stopped it in the second round. His next opponent, Russian Gennadiy Shatkov, had won the gold medal in the middleweight division at the 1956 Olympic Games, but Clay won by a unanimous points decision, 5-0. In the semifinals he also beat Tony Madigan of Australia by a 5-0 unanimous points decision.

In the 178-pound (80 kilograms) division final, Clay faced Zbigniew Pietrzykowski of Poland. The Pole gave Clay trouble in the opening round, landing solid punches to take the early lead in the fight. The second round was pretty even, so Clay knew he needed a strong third and

SIGNS OF STARDOM

Prior to the Games, many had picked Clay as one of the top contenders for the United States to win a boxing medal. He had put together a stunning amateur career, which included 100 wins in 108 bouts while winning back-to-back Golden Gloves titles in 1959 and 1960. He also won the National Amateur Athletic Union light heavyweight in those 2 years.

final round to win gold—and he delivered. He battered the Polish fighter with punishing blows; he drew blood; and he came close to knocking him out before the bell sounded. The final-round rally earned Clay an Olympic gold medal and gave the world a glimpse at his growing greatness.

> "He who is not courageous enough to take risks will accomplish nothing in life."
> – Cassius Clay

OVERCOMING AEROPHOBIA

Clay was afraid of flying, and after he had a rough flight from Louisville to California for the Olympic trials, he was dead set against flying all the way to Rome for the Olympic Games. He inquired about taking a ship, but there was no time for that. It took a long talk from a boxing trainer who first suggested the sport to him when he was 12 to finally convince Clay to get on the airplane to Rome.

IT JUST TAKES ONE
FIRST AMERICAN ALL-AROUND GOLD

Los Angeles 1984: Gymnastics

The world of women's gymnastics was flipped upside down in the summer of 1984, when a power-packing, 4-foot 9-inch bundle of pure athleticism by the name of Mary Lou Retton grabbed American hearts and didn't let go during a glorious stretch of stunning performances. The 16-year-old, who idolized legendary gymnast Nadia Comăneci growing up, became the first U.S. woman to win an Olympic all-around gold medal.

When the women's gymnastics event got under way at Pauley Pavilion in the UCLA campus, Romania's Ecaterina Szabo was the popular pick to win the all-around gold medal, and with good reason. Besides being the reigning world champion on the floor exercise, she was also second in the vault and uneven bars at the World Championships.

Trailing Szabo (who won more gold medals than any athlete in the 1984 Games) and heading into her final all-around event—the vault—Retton struck and stuck her landing to earn a perfect 10 and burst into the history books by nudging Szabo off the gold medal podium by 0.05 points. This was the only event in which the dynamic Szabo did not win the gold. It was a spectacular display by Retton. She had undergone arthroscopic surgery to remove torn cartilage in her right knee less than eight weeks before the Olympics and questions swirled if she

EASTERN BLOC BOYCOTT

The 1984 Olympics were missing many talented athletes from Eastern Bloc nations due to a Soviet-led boycott done in apparent retaliation for the U.S.-led boycott of the 1980 Olympics in Moscow. Romania chose to ignore the boycott and participate in the Los Angeles Olympics.

would even be able to compete. Retton also won silver medals in the vault and team event and bronze medals in the uneven bars and floor exercise.

> "You give up your childhood. You miss proms and games and high-school events, and people say it's awful... I say it was a good trade. You miss something but I think I gained more than I lost."
> – Mary Lou Retton

FOLLOWING HER FOOTSTEPS

Retton was inducted into the International Gymnastics Hall of Fame in 1997, and today is the proud mom of four daughters who compete in the sport. Her eldest, Shayla Kelley, was on the Acrobatics and Tumbling team at Baylor University. Retton's second eldest, McKenna Kelley, competed as a gymnast at the NCAA Division I level while attending Louisiana State University.

INAUGURAL GOLD
FIRST MODERN ERA CHAMP CROWNED

Athens 1896: Track and Field

When the Olympic Games were resuscitated in 1896 following a more than 1,500-year hiatus—they were abolished in 393 A.D. by Emperor Theodosius I—American James Connolly was willing to make a huge sacrifice to participate in them. The 27-year-old Harvard University freshman was the reigning national champion in the hop, step, and jump (these days known as the triple jump), but when he asked school officials if he could represent Harvard at the Olympics he was informed he'd have to resign his spot on campus and he might not be able to get it back when he returned—so he quit.

He raised travel money and joined most of the U.S. squad for an arduous crossing of the Atlantic Ocean that took more than two weeks. Connolly trained as much as he could on the deck with his teammates during the trip.

Legend has it that a thief grabbed his wallet shortly after landing in Naples, Italy, and Connolly chased him down to get it back.

Upon arriving in Athens, he discovered that his event was going to lead off the Olympics the next day following the opening ceremonies rather than later in the competition, which was what he had expected.

The Summer Olympics: Greatest Moments

GREAT LEAPER, PROLIFIC WRITER

Connolly traveled to France in 1900 to attempt to defend his title at the Olympic Games in Paris, but he finished second to his American teammate Meyer Prinstein. In 1904 he was in St. Louis, Missouri, for the next Olympics, but he wasn't jumping. He attended as a journalist and would go on to write numerous books and short stories during his career.

Apparently, having little time to acclimate to land after being at sea didn't affect him, as he leaped 44.98 feet (13.71 meters) to outjump his nearest competitor by more than 3 feet and become the first Olympic champion of the modern era. He also placed second in the high jump and third in the long jump.

Connolly returned to the Olympics at Paris in 1900. He was less successful there, but still managed to win a silver in the triple jump, giving him four career Olympic medals.

DROPPED AT SEA

More than 230 athletes participated in the 1896 Olympics. For some of the swimming races, competitors were taken out to sea by boat and had to swim the required distance back to shore.

FASTEST WOMAN IN THE WORLD
FLO-JO TROUNCES THE 200-METER MAR

Seoul 1988: Track and Field

Florence Griffith-Joyner stormed into Seoul for the 1988 Summer Olympics, dominated two of track and field's most treasured events, and departed as the fastest woman on the planet. She blitzed the field, handily winning both the 100- and 200-meter sprints, and she pulled it off in record fashion.

Two months before the Olympics, Flo-Jo, as she was known, ran a head-turning, world-record time of 10.49 seconds in winning the 100 meters at the U.S. trials in Indianapolis. She nearly duplicated that time in Seoul, blasting a 10.54 to win gold and break Evelyn Ashford's Olympic record time of 10.97 seconds that she had set 4 years earlier in Los Angeles. Ashford was second in Seoul with a time of 10.83 seconds.

The real moment of her Games came in the 200 meters. Flo-Jo ran a lethal race. Rounding the turn heading into the final 80 meters of the race, her long stride gobbled up the track and propelled her to another victory, this one with a world-record time of 21.34 seconds. That smashed the world record of 21.71 seconds previously owned by East Germany's Marita Koch, and it was nearly a half-second better than the Olympic record of 21.81 seconds that

SKEPTICISM IN SEOUL

Some competitors openly suspected Flo-Jo of using performance-enhancing substances because of her dramatic improvements during the previous year, but she maintained she never used them. A male sprinter told a magazine she paid him for human growth hormone, which she denied. She also tested negative on all her drug tests.

Valerie Brisco-Hooks ran at the 1984 Games in Los Angeles. Griffith-Joyner also won a third gold running a leg on the 4x100-meter relay and a silver in the 4x400-meter relay.

Just how good was Flo-Jo in the summer of 1988? Both her world records in the 100 and 200 meters still stand today.

> "I believe in the impossible because no one else does."
> – Florence Griffith-Joyner

TRAGIC PASSING

Griffith-Joyner died suddenly and unexpectedly at age thirty-eight. Asleep in bed at her home, she suffered a severe epileptic seizure, which caused her to be suffocated by her bedding. Epilepsy is a neurological disorder caused by the disruption of nerve function in the brain. The condition affects about 2.5 million Americans.

INDIGENOUS INTENT
FREEMAN DELIVERS FOR HER PEOPLE

Sydney 2000: Track and Field

On the evening of September 25, 2000, the Olympic Stadium in Sydney was a cauldron of emotion, brimming with hope and plenty of frayed nerves, as the competitors for the women's 400-meter finals settled into the starting blocks. In lane 6 was Australian Cathy Freeman, the lone runner who was zippered into a body suit, one she had worn throughout the preliminary rounds. The vast majority of the more than 112,000 spectators on hand were there to cheer her to victory.

Ten days earlier Freeman had the honor of lighting the Olympic flame during the opening ceremonies, and now the beloved Australian of Aboriginal descent prepared for one time around the track to fulfill a dream for both her and a nation. Her unique racing suit was bathed in silver, yellow, and green for her country; Freeman's racing shoes of red, yellow, and black were a nod to her Aboriginal heritage.

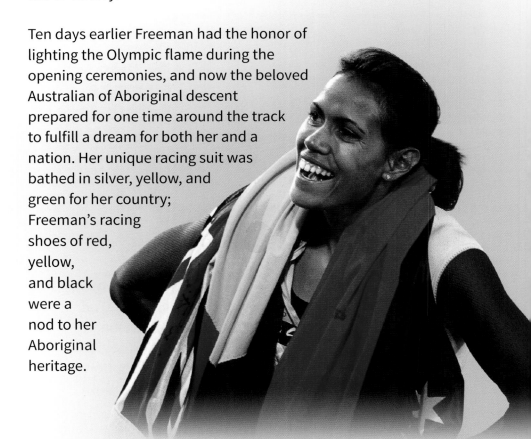

In a field chock-full of world-class speed, the last turn was congested with several runners eyeing a gold medal finish. It was here, in the final 100 meters of the race, that Freeman separated herself to hit the tape with a winning time of 49.11 seconds while fans roared in approval. Jamaica's Lorraine Graham and Great Britain's Katharine Merry took the silver and bronze, respectively. Freeman did a victory lap barefoot, proudly carrying both the Australian and Aboriginal flags, and her performance is one that still resonates in the country all these years later.

"I felt the track under the very tips of my toes and I'll never forget that I felt like I was being carried, like a surfer on a wave."

– Cathy Freeman

Cathy Freeman wins the gold medal in the 400-meter run at the 2000 Olympics in her home country of Australia.

PRIZE MATCHES THE SHOES JOHNSON SETS 200 METERS RECORD

Atlanta 1996: Track and Field

Michael Johnson made a grand entry into the Olympic record books during the 1996 Summer Games in Atlanta, becoming the only man to ever win gold in both the 200 and 400 meters at a single Olympics. And he did it wearing golden spikes that matched the magnitude of the moment, locking down his place among the greatest sprinters of all time.

The historic moment came with the appropriate sizzle, as Johnson demolished his own world record in the 200-meter final, blazing to a time of 19.32 seconds that chopped more than three-tenths of a second off the record of 19.66 he had set just six weeks earlier at the Olympic Trials. Johnson conquered a ferocious field in Atlanta, which included Frankie Fredericks of Namibia who had beaten him a couple of months earlier to snap his 22-race winning streak. Johnson's world record stood for a dozen years before Usain Bolt of Jamaica lowered it to a staggering 19.19 seconds.

Three days earlier from lane four in the 400-meter final, Johnson continued his decade of dominance in the event by winning gold with an Olympic record time of 43.49 seconds. The next closest to him was Roger Black of Great Britain in 44.91 seconds. Beginning in 1993, Johnson had a stretch where he went unbeaten in fifty-eight 400-meter races in a row, and Atlanta was just a continuation of his stranglehold on the event. Three years later Johnson would run a world-record time of 43.18 seconds, a mark that would hold up for 17 years.

"It wasn't the perfect race, but it was absolutely the best race I ever ran."
— Michael Johnson

Michael Johnson wins the 400-meter run at the 1996 Olympics in Atlanta, completing the first half of his historic double that also included a gold medal in the 200 meters.

UNDIVIDED ATTENTION
KOREAS WALK IN UNDER SAME FLAG

Sydney 2000: Opening Ceremonies

There were numerous world and Olympic records broken during the 2000 Summer Games in Sydney, but among all the numbers-busting moments that took place, one of the most memorable occurred *before* the events even began. The historic highlight happened during the opening ceremony at the Olympic Stadium during the procession of nations where all the athletes walk in together following their country's flag.

Athletes from North and South Korea, two nations who were still officially at war, walked into the stadium together with a sign that read "Korea" and a flag depicting the Korean peninsula, which was known as the "unification flag." Many of the Koreans had their hands joined and their arms raised, and when the public address announcer announced that these two nations were marching together there was hearty cheering from the crowd.

North Korea operates under a communist dictatorship, while South Korea is a democratic Republic. Residing between the two countries is the famous demilitarized zone, which separates the two. Through the years this has been some of the most hostile terrain in the world, but in recent years both countries have made great efforts to reduce tensions.

The day after the opening ceremonies, with the events beginning, the two countries

CARRYING THE FLAG OF UNIFICATION

Carrying your country's flag in the opening ceremony of an Olympics is a giant honor for an athlete, so when North and South Korea marched into the Olympic Stadium one athlete from each country was chosen to hold the unification flag: Park Chong Chul, a male judo coach from North Korea, and Chung Un Soon, a female basketball player from South Korea.

competed under their own flags. But for one special evening the Olympics brought people together and the world saw the power of sports in uniting nations and promoting peace.

> **"Many considered it an impossible dream to have an Olympics of peace, in which North Korea would participate and the two Koreas would form a joint team."**
> **– Moon Jae-in, South Korean president**

BREAKING BARRIERS

The delegation of athletes from North and South Korea traveled together from the athletes' village to the stadium on the same buses, and they spent hours speaking with each other throughout the historic evening.

CARL THE CONQUEROR
LEWIS WINS RELAY TO MATCH OWENS

Los Angeles 1984: Track and Field

The great Jesse Owens' record performance of four gold medals in track and field at the 1936 Berlin Games had been tucked away on the top shelf of history, unreachable for nearly half a century, until Carl Lewis duplicated the extraordinary feat in the Los Angeles sunshine at the 1984 Games. He captured gold medals in the same four events Owens had.

Lewis' plunge into history began with the 100 meters, the event thought to present the stiffest competition of the four. He posted the fastest time of all competitors in the semis and ran a strong 9.99 to win gold in the finals. The next day he was first to the finish line in both of his 200-meter heats and in the evening competed in his favorite event, the long jump. He posted a leap of 28 feet and ¼ inch (8.30 meters) on his first jump, which in the windy conditions at the L.A. Coliseum proved good enough for his second gold medal. Lewis was then the first of three Americans to the tape to lead a clean sweep of the 200-meter final.

The big moment came when Lewis ran the anchor leg for the U.S. team in the 4x100-meter relay. The Americans were the clear favorites, but one bad handoff could negate their superior speed in the short

LEGENDARY LONG JUMPER

Only Lewis has won the long jump at four consecutive Olympic Games. He dueled with Mike Powell at the Atlanta Games in 1996. Powell, runner-up to Lewis in 1998 and 1992, broke Bob Beamon's 23-year old world-record in 1991. In Atlanta, Lewis leaped 8.50 meters to win a fourth long jump gold medal. Powell finished fifth and never beat Lewis at the Olympics.

race. The race went smoothly, however, and Lewis' split of 8.94 seconds helped the Americans win gold with a world-record time of 37.83 seconds. Lewis ran back up the track to celebrate the first track and field world record of those Games with his teammates.

> **"You have to free your mind to do things you wouldn't think of doing. Don't ever say no."**
> **– Carl Lewis**

GOLDEN KEEPSAKE

Lewis' father, Bill, passed away due to cancer in 1987. Lewis buried him with the gold medal Carl won in the 100 meters at the 1984 Los Angeles Games. Lewis has said many times that his father was the motivation for his success at the 1988 Olympics in Seoul. Lewis won two more gold medals at those Games, including another for winning the 100 meters.

DANGEROUS DIVE LOUGANIS RECOVERS TO WIN AGAIN

Seoul 1988: Men's Diving

Greg Louganis delivered a diving career filled with jaw-dropping displays of aerial excellence, twisting, flipping, and somersaulting his way straight to the Olympic Hall of Fame and staking a tough-to-dispute claim as the greatest diver of all time. However, the four-time Olympic gold medalist is most often remembered for a dive that went dangerously wrong—and how the moment evolved to define his greatness in the sport.

At the 1988 Summer Games in Seoul, South Korea, Louganis was cruising through the preliminary round of the 3-meter springboard diving event, leading the field after eight of 11 rounds. On his ninth dive,

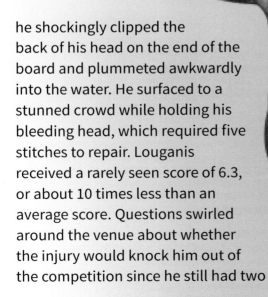

he shockingly clipped the back of his head on the end of the board and plummeted awkwardly into the water. He surfaced to a stunned crowd while holding his bleeding head, which required five stitches to repair. Louganis received a rarely seen score of 6.3, or about 10 times less than an average score. Questions swirled around the venue about whether the injury would knock him out of the competition since he still had two

SEOUL SECRET

When Louganis arrived in Seoul for the Summer Games he was competing with a secret: 6 months earlier he had been diagnosed as HIV-positive and thought he was dying. Gripped by fear, he didn't tell USA team doctor James Puffer about his condition as Puffer was stitching his head up without using latex gloves. Years later Louganis apologized to Puffer.

more dives remaining, including one within 30 minutes.

Nursing a concussion and rattled confidence, Louganis huddled with Ron O'Brien, his long-time coach. They decided he had worked too hard to quit, and he climbed back on the board and nailed his next dive, earning the top score of any diver in the preliminary round. The following day Louganis put on a sensational performance to win gold.

REPEAT PERFORMANCE

When Louganis repeated his Los Angeles Games golden double four years later in Seoul, he became the first man in Olympic history to sweep the diving events in consecutive Olympic Games.

HISTORIC SCORE
NADIA SCORES A PERFECT 10

Montreal 1976: Gymnastics

In the span of just a couple of minutes during the opening day of the women's gymnastics competition at the 1976 Olympics, a 14-year-old from Romania launched herself into history and became one of those iconic gymnasts recognizable by first name only: Mary Lou, Gabby, Simone, and Nadia.

Nadia Comăneci delivered a flawless performance on the uneven bars during the compulsory round, earning the first perfect 10 in Olympic history. The scoreboard wasn't designed to handle the historical occasion though, so the best it could do was display 1.00. This created confusion throughout the arena that eventually turned into cheering when the crowd realized that it had witnessed something that had never been done before.

As it turned out, Comăneci was just getting started. The next night she got another 10 on the uneven bars *and* a 10 on the balance beam. Later in the competition, more 10s followed and by the time the teen left Montreal she had seven of them: four on the uneven bars and three on the balance beam.

Comăneci was the breakout star of these games. She took home five medals, the most precious of which was a gold in the all-around competition, where she became the youngest to ever do so, as

NADIA'S NUPTIALS

In 1996, in Bucharest, Romania, Comăneci married Bart Conner, a two-time U.S. men's Olympic gold medalist. They first met 20 years earlier, just months before Comăneci became a worldwide celebrity in Montreal. Their wedding was broadcast live across her home country. The couple now operates a gymnastics school in Norman, Oklahoma.

well as the first Romanian. Thanks to her bundle of 10s she also won gold medals on the balance beam and uneven bars. Overall, Comăneci won five gold and nine career Olympic medals, but decades later she is still best remembered for that first perfect moment.

> "Enjoy the journey and try to get better every day. And don't lose the passion and the love for what you do."
> — Nadia Comăneci

NEVER AGAIN

The 10-point scoring system was ditched in 2006 for an open-ended system, which means perfect 10s are no longer attainable in gymnastics. The new scoring system uses two separate judging panels and a mathematical formula to determine a score that considers difficulty, artistry, and execution. The top world-class gymnasts score between 15 and 16 under the new system.

FACING DOWN FASCISM
OWENS WINS GOLD AS HITLER WATCHES

Berlin 1936: Track and Field

German dictator Adolph Hitler hoped the 1936 Summer Olympics in Berlin would prove his polluted theory of racial supremacy, but African-American track standout Jesse Owens instead seized the spotlight from the monster (who would soon be responsible for killing millions of innocent people) and put on a performance still raved about more than 75 years later.

Owens won a gold medal in his first event, the 100 meters, by equaling the world record of 10.3 seconds. The German competitor in the race, Erich Borchmeyer, finished a distant fifth. The United States took silver as well, as Ralph Metcalfe, also African-American, finished second. Legend has it that Hitler snubbed Owens that day, even though the crowd cheered his victory. In reality, Hitler had stopped greeting winners after day one of competition. Although Germany by far won the most medals of any nation at these Games, Hitler could not have been happy that Aryan superiority had been soundly exposed as a myth.

Owens' march to Olympic history continued with a win over Germany's Luz Long in the long jump competition the

A FABULOUS 45 MINUTES

In the amount of time it takes to stream a couple of sitcoms on your tablet, Jesse Owens put on one of the greatest athletic performances ever. At the 1935 Big Ten Track and Field Championships, he tied the world record in the 100-yard dash and then set the world record in the long jump, the 220-yard dash, and the 220-yard low hurdles. And he did it all in a 45-minute span.

following day. He then set another world record in later winning the 200 meters in 20.7 seconds. He capped off his golden blitz in Berlin by running the opening leg on the victorious U.S. 4x100-meter relay team that broke the world record. Owens became the first American to win four gold medals in track and field at a single Olympics, a mark that remained untouchable for 48 years.

LEGAL DISCRIMINATION

Several U.S. politicians wanted to boycott the Berlin Games to protest Germany's discriminatory policies against Jews. Ultimately, Owens was allowed to shine. Ironically, he returned home to a nation that practiced legalized discrimination against him for 30 more years.

GOLDEN GREAT
PHELPS WINS EIGHT GOLD MEDALS

Beijing 2008: Swimming

The plan that was hatched prior to the 2008 Summer Olympics was so absurd that it was knocking on the door of the impossible. It entailed attempting to win eight swimming gold medals in eight events, a feat unprecedented in any sport in the history of the Summer Games.

Who could be capable of pulling off such a caper? The one and only Michael Phelps, the greatest swimmer who has ever lived. After winning six gold medals and two bronze medals at the 2004 Summer Olympics in Athens, his appetite was clearly whetted to do more, much more, in Beijing. And he turned what seemed like an impossible challenge into a showcase of his greatness by winning all eight of those races.

He carved up the water every time he entered the pool, setting— are you ready for this stat?—seven world records and one Olympic record (100-meter butterfly). His individual world records came in the 200-meter butterfly, 200-meter freestyle, 200-meter individual

medley, and 400-meter individual medley (he still holds this record); and his relay wins came in the 4x100-meter freestyle relay, the 4x200-meter freestyle relay, and 4x100-meter medley relay.

Over the course of 9 days, Phelps swam 17 races, which included eight finals (five individual and three relays), along with preliminaries and semis. He swam more than 30 miles of races at the National Aquatics Center, the bulk of those out in front of the field, as he turned in the greatest performance ever seen in a single Olympics.

"**Everything was accomplished. I will have the medals forever.**"

– Michael Phelps

Phelps won a record-setting eight gold medals at the 2008 Summer Olympics in Beijing.

ETERNAL FRIENDSHIP
POLE VAULTERS REFUSE TO COMPETE

Berlin 1936: Track and Field

Two Japanese pole vaulters, disappointed by how officials chose to break a tie between them at the 1936 Olympics in Berlin, turned to a jeweler in their country for some creative assistance that catapulted them into Olympic lore forever. Shuhei Nishida and Sueo Oe, teammates and close friends, were locked in a duel for the silver medal in the men's pole vault. American Earle Meadows had secured the gold by clearing 4 meters 35 centimeters (14.27 feet), a height the two Japanese pole vaulters, along with American Bill Sefton, were unable to conquer. When Sefton missed at 4.25 meters (13.94 feet)—which both Nishida and Oe cleared—they were guaranteed medals. The two friends wanted to share the honor of being second and declined to continue, as they didn't want to compete against each other. Olympic officials refused their request and told Japanese team officials to decide who should get the silver and bronze medals. After a long discussion Nishida was chosen for the silver since he cleared 4.25 meters on his first attempt while it took Oe two tries to find success.

POST-COMPETITION YEARS

Nishida was actively involved in sports after retiring from competition. In 1959 he was appointed president of the Japanese Athletics Federation, and later he had the distinction of becoming an Honorary Vice-President, as well as a member of the Japanese Olympic Committee. Oe was killed in World War II at the Battle of Wake Island in December of 1941.

The friends, unhappy with the decision, returned home and took their medals to a jeweler who cut them both in half and fused them to form two new medals, each featuring half silver and half bronze. These became known as The Medals of Eternal Friendship.

Oe's medal is on display at the National Museum in Tokyo. His family donated it after he was killed in action during WWII in 1941.

ANOTHER MEDAL

At the 1932 Summer Games in Los Angeles, Nishida won his first Olympic silver medal in the pole vault, which was contested at the Los Angeles Memorial Coliseum. Bill Miller of the United States won gold and George Jefferson, also from the United States, took home the bronze medal.

READY OR NOT
REFUGEE ATHLETES' FIRST GAMES

Rio 2016: Opening Ceremonies

Every athlete's dream of performing on the Olympic stage is filled with challenges along the way, but for a special group of 10 who competed in Rio at the 2016 Games, how they got to the Olympics—and what they endured in doing so—was beyond extraordinary. Near the end of 2015, IOC President Thomas Bach announced the creation of the Refugee Olympic Team, something that had never been a part of any Olympic Games, to send a beautiful message of hope, care, and the opportunity to compete in Olympics, to millions of refugees worldwide.

A total of 10 refugee athletes from Ethiopia, Syria, South Sudan, and the Democratic Republic of Congo (DRC) were chosen to compete. Among the group were swimmers, judokas, medium-distance runners, and a marathoner. Each of them carried memories of horrific experiences in their lives when they came to Rio. For example, Yiech Pur Biel of South Sudan lived in a refugee camp in Kenya for 10 years

LIFE-SAVING SWIMMER

In the summer of 2015, swimmer Yusra Mardini fled her home in war-ravaged Syria. To cross the Mediterranean Sea she got in a flimsy dinghy with 20 others, hoping to reach Greece. With too much weight in a boat capable of holding only a few, it began taking on water. For more than three hours Mardini swam and helped every person get safely to shore.

to escape civil war in his country; Rami Anis, facing the threat of being blown up or kidnapped in his home country of Syria, fled to Turkey and eventually received asylum in Belgium; and Yolande Mabika, separated from her family at a young age, escaped civil war in the Democratic Republic of Congo and went to Brazil, where she lived in a center for displaced children.

While no refugee athlete took home a medal, their presence at the events was uplifting, their efforts were loudly cheered and supported by spectators, and they fortified what the Olympic spirit is all about.

A FLAG FOR ALL

The members of the Refugee Olympic Team competed in Rio under the flag of the International Olympic Committee. At the Opening Ceremonies, South Sudanese refugee Rose Lokonyen, an 800-meter runner, was the flag bearer. Judoka Popole Mesenga of the DRC carried the flag to close the Games.

GREATEST RACE EVER RUN
RUDISHA IS FASTEST OF THE FAST

London 2012: Track and Field

When the runners gathered for the finals of the 800 meters at the 2012 Olympics in London, they had no idea that what they were about to do would link them in history as part of what many now refer to as the greatest race ever run. Indeed, this festival of speed had everything. For starters, Kenya's David Rudisha grabbed the lead in the first turn and ran a merciless pace the rest of the way in breaking his own world record by clocking a 1:40.91. His early race splits were lung-searing and bordered on unbelievable. No wonder he had only been beaten once in his past 46 races.

Beyond Rudisha's record gold medal performance, what was astounding about this race is that every runner in the field set a national record or a personal or season's best. The silver medal went to 18-year-old Nijel Amos of Botswana, the reigning world junior champion, whose time of 1:41.73 was more than a second faster than he had ever run before. Timothy Kitum, a 17-year-old from Kenya, also improved his personal-best time by a whopping 1.41 seconds to take the bronze medal in 1:42.53. Great Britain's Andrew Osagie finished last in the eight-man field, running 1:43.77. That time would have won the 800 meters at all of the previous three Olympics.

Duane Solomon and Nick Symmonds of the United States ran marvelous races, becoming just the second and third Americans to run under 1:43, but they just missed out on medals. Solomon was fourth in 1:42.82 and Symmonds took fifth in 1:42.95.

"I've waited for this moment for a very long time. To come here and get a world record is unbelievable. I had no doubt about winning. Today the weather was beautiful—I decided to go for it."

– David Rudisha

Kenya's David Rudisha clocked a world record in the finals of the 800-meter run at the 2012 Summer Olympics in London in a race where everyone in the field ran a personal or season's best time.

MIRACLE ON THE MAT
RULON GARDNER WINS GOLD

Sydney 2000: Greco-Roman Wrestling

Alexander Karelin spent much of his lifetime ruling the Greco-Roman wrestling world by bullying opponents on his march to greatness. Arriving in Sydney for the 2000 Summer Games the Russian with the chiseled physique and menacing stare had won three consecutive Olympic gold medals, hadn't been beaten in 13 years, and surrendered points about as often as a solar eclipse occurs.

That dominating form was on full display right from the opening match in the heavyweight division in Sydney. Karelin didn't give up a point in any of his matches as he cruised into the finals, where he appeared poised to become just the third athlete to ever win Olympic gold in the same event four consecutive times.

Awaiting him in the finals was American Rulon Gardner, who wasn't expected to even make it this far. In fact, the 29-year-old had narrowly escaped with a 3–2 win in the semifinals over Israel's Yuri Evseihik. No one gave Gardner much of a chance to dethrone the great Karelin, especially since in their only meeting the Russian handily won 5–0.

This match, however, rocked the wrestling landscape and turned out to be one of the biggest upsets in Olympic history, as Gardner was able to dodge Karelin's lethal reverse body lift, a move that had crushed a lengthy list of opponents through the years. After a scoreless opening period, Gardner broke free from Karelin's clinch in the second period for the only point that would be scored in an epic 1–0 victory.

"**When did I think I could beat him? About 10 minutes ago. I kept saying, 'I think I can. I think I can.' But it wasn't until it was over that I knew I could.**"

– Rulon Gardner

Rulon Gardner did the unthinkable at the 2000 Summer Olympics in Sydney, ending the reign of Russia's Alexander Karelin in Greco-Roman wrestling with a stunning 1–0 victory.

LEAN ON ME
RUNNER FINISHES WITH DAD'S HELP

Barcelona 1992: Track and Field

The true spirit of the Olympic Games can often be found in the most unlikely spots. In 1992, it was on the backstretch of a semifinal race in the men's 400-meter run at the Olympic Stadium in Barcelona. It was there where Great Britain's Derek Redmond crumpled to the track with a torn right hamstring midway through his heat.

Despite suffering horrific physical pain, and the crushing reality that his dream of Olympic gold was done, he summoned remarkable courage and strength to get up and finish the race. He began slowly hobbling around the track on one leg. The crowd began rising to its feet to encourage him, and when he neared the last turn his father bolted out of the stands, weaved around security guards, and put his arms around his son to help him get to the finish line. Meanwhile, 65,000 fans now in full voice cheered Redmond on, and he allowed his tears of bitter disappointment to flow in the comfort of his father's embrace. Although he did cross the finish line, because he had his father's assistance, Redmond was officially disqualified.

Redmond had been running well prior to the injury. In the preliminary heats, his time of 45.03 seconds was the fastest of anyone in the field, and in the quarterfinals he won his heat with a time of 45.02. While he didn't experience the thrill of having an Olympic medal hung around his neck, he showed the world what it means to be an Olympian by always doing your best and never giving up.

> "The old man put his arms around me and said, 'Look, you don't need to do this. You can stop now, you haven't got nothing to prove.' And I said, 'Oh, I have — now get me back into Lane 5. I want to finish.'"
>
> **– Derek Redmond**

Derek Redmond's father comes out of the stands to help his son finish his 400-meter race after sustaining an injury at the 1992 Summer Olympics in Barcelona.

CANADIAN KINDNESS
SAILOR PULLS TWO MEN FROM SEA

Seoul 1988: Sailing

Through the years the water is where some of the most memorable moments in Summer Olympic history have occurred, delivered by athletes whose careers are often decided by hundredths of seconds while millions around the globe watch the agony and ecstasy unfold. Yet one of the Summer Games' signature moments involving water didn't take place during a live prime time television broadcast. There were also no cheering crowds or records set.

But two lives were saved in heroic fashion.

Canadian Lawrence Lemieux was competing in sailing in the individual event (Finn class) at the 1988 Games in Seoul and was in prime position for a medal as he navigated his way through stomach-turning seas and brutal winds sweeping off the coast. Lemieux was in second place and halfway through the fifth of the seven races when he encountered a capsized boat involved in a different race. One man was clinging to the overturned boat while the other was in the water and being swept away from it.

Lemieux quickly abandoned his hope of winning a medal and rescued the two men from Singapore, Joseph Chan and Siew Shaw Her. He waited for help to arrive—a Korean Navy boat brought them to shore—and then he resumed his race, still finishing 22nd out of 32 boats. Although Lemieux didn't medal, he was presented with the International Olympic Committee's (IOC) prestigious Pierre de Coubertin medal. It is awarded to those who exemplify the spirit of sportsmanship in the Olympics.

> **"I could have won gold. But, in the same circumstances, I would do what I did again."**
>
> **"The first rule of sailing is you see someone in trouble you help him."**
> **– Lawrence Lemieux**

Canadian Lawrence Lemieux gave up his bid for a gold medal to rescue two men during the 1988 Summer Olympics.

HERCULEAN HOIST
SOVIET STRONGMAN SETS RECORD

Montreal 1976: Weightlifting

In the 1970s, the Soviet Union's Vasily Alekseyev was a one-man show of unimaginable strength and unusual training methods. Shunning coaches, training solo and putting himself through twice-a-day lifting sessions at all hours of the day and night, Alekseyev hoisted weights that left spectators in awe—and competitors usually vying for second place.

With 345 pounds on his 6-foot 1-inch frame, Alekseyev showed up in Montreal for the 1976 Summer Games as the defending champion in the super heavyweight division, having won gold in Munich in 1972. Plus, he hadn't been beaten since 1970.

During the clean and jerk at the Montreal Games, the crowd watched in silence as Alekseyev focused on preparing to lift what would be a world-record 562 pounds (255 kilograms) over his head. In the clean and jerk, lifters must bring the barbell from the floor up to shoulder height and then raise the bar over their head while standing upright and displaying control of the bar for the judges. As Alekseyev got the bar to his shoulders, spectators began cheering in approval. Off to the side of the stage, Soviet judges were motioning for quiet. Seconds later he pushed the massive weight above his head while

The Summer Olympics: Greatest Moments

his legs shook from the stress of the lift. Once Alekseyev demonstrated control the judge signaled it was a successful lift and the crowd thundered its approval of watching a Herculean hoist. Alekseyev set 80 world records in his career.

"Every time I see myself in the mirror I almost feel like asking myself for an autograph."

– Vasily Alekseyev

Alekseyev set a world record with this lift of 507 pounds (230 kilograms) in the clean and press.

HALL WORTHY

Alekseyev was inducted into the International Weightlifting Federation Hall of Fame in 1993.

ALL POWER TO THE PEOPLE
SPRINTERS PROTEST ON THE PODIUM

Mexico City 1968: Track and Field

In the lead up to the 1968 Summer Olympics, American sprinters Tommie Smith and John Carlos had grown frustrated by the plodding pace of the Civil Rights movement and the social injustices occurring across the country, and they saw the Games as an opportunity to push for a change. Prior to arriving in Mexico City they had helped organize the Olympic Project for Human Rights (OPHR), whose goals included better treatment for both black athletes and people worldwide.

When Smith won the 200-meter finals with a world-record time of 19.83 seconds, with Carlos winning bronze (20.10), they had their platform to both receive their medals and make a statement to the world. They stood on the podium wearing black socks without shoes to bring attention to poverty, beads around their necks to protest lynching, and black gloves on the one fist each raised to represent their solidarity and support of both black Americans and oppressed people worldwide. Australian silver medalist Peter Norman, who suggested the Americans share the gloves after Carlos forgot his, wore an OPHR badge to show his support for the Americans.

Spectators, upset that a medal ceremony was turned into a political statement, hurled angry insults. Officials rushed them out of the stadium, they were expelled from the Olympic Village, and when they returned to the United States they faced backlash and death threats. More than 50 years later, their gesture remains one of the Games' iconic moments.

> "If I win, I am American, not a black American. But if I did something bad, then they would say I am a Negro. We are black and we are proud of being black. Black America will understand what we did tonight."
>
> **– Tommie Smith**

Tommie Smith and John Carlos display a Black Power salute on the medal podium at the 1968 Summer Olympics in Mexico City to bring attention to social injustice worldwide.

SURVIVOR'S SWIM
SURVIVOR BEATS CANCER AND WINS

Beijing 2008: Swimming

Maarten van der Weijden's journey to Olympic glory involved much more than enduring the grueling practices that are a part of the regimens of long-distance swimmers. Diagnosed with acute leukemia in 2001, and given just a small chance at survival, the great Dutch champion dug in and fought for his life. Forced to deal with long hospital stays, several rounds of chemotherapy, and a stem cell transplant, he remarkably snatched his health back and returned to competitive swimming two years later.

In 2006, van der Weijden began showing signs of returning to the championship form that his disease had robbed him of by winning a silver medal in the 10 kilometers (6.2 miles) at the European Championships. When he then won the 25 kilometers (15.5 miles) at the 2008 Open Water World Championships in Seville, Spain, he was primed for the Beijing Olympics later that year.

At the Shunyi Olympic Rowing-Canoeing Park, the venue for the inaugural 10-kilometer open water marathon race at the Beijing Olympics, van der Weijden found himself in a three-way race to the

FIGHTING CANCER

In 2015 van der Weijden conducted his first annual "Swim to Fight Cancer" event in Den Bosch, Netherlands. More than 500 participants took part in the swim to raise more than $530,000 for cancer research. He has also swam the running marathon distance of 26 miles and 385 yards as a fund-raiser to fight cancer. In 2018 he raised almost $5.3 million.

finish line down the stretch with David Davies of Great Britain and Germany's Thomas Lurz. It was Davies who led most of the race by several body lengths in a downpour, but van der Weijden out-swam him over the final few hundred meters to win with a time of 1:51:51.6. Davies missed out on the gold by a narrow 1.5 seconds, while Lurz took the bronze medal, 2 seconds behind van der Weijden at 1:51:53.6.

FOUNDATION FUNDS

In 2017, van der Weijden established the Maarten van der Weijden Foundation with the goal to "raise funds for the interests of patients with cancer."

Each year, the foundation selects new cancer research projects and/or studies to support. In 2019, the foundation donated to 15 different projects from developing CAR-T cell therapy to detecting heart damage in children due to cancer treatment.

BEGINNER'S LUCK
TEENAGER MATHIAS WINS DECATHLON

London 1948: Decathlon

Bob Mathias barged onto the international track and field scene at the incredibly young age of 17, thanks to a high school coach's encouraging words, some good study habits, and a lethal combination of strength and speed rarely seen at that age. In the spring of his senior year (1948), Mathias' high school track coach in Tulare, California, suggested that he should try decathlon, the grueling 10-event test staged over two days that determines the world's greatest athlete.

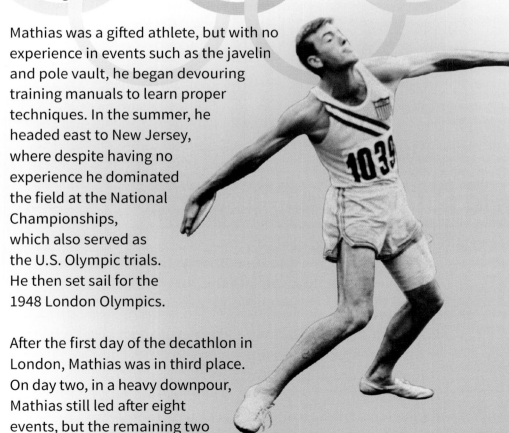

Mathias was a gifted athlete, but with no experience in events such as the javelin and pole vault, he began devouring training manuals to learn proper techniques. In the summer, he headed east to New Jersey, where despite having no experience he dominated the field at the National Championships, which also served as the U.S. Olympic trials. He then set sail for the 1948 London Olympics.

After the first day of the decathlon in London, Mathias was in third place. On day two, in a heavy downpour, Mathias still led after eight events, but the remaining two

PERFORMING IN POLITICS

Following his athletic career, a stint with the Marines, and acting in half a dozen movies, Mathias went into politics. He served four terms as a Republican congressman for California, where he grew up. He later served as director of the U.S. Olympic Training Center and he oversaw the National Fitness Foundation.

events—javelin and 1,500-meter run—were not his strongest.

After a respectable 11th place result in javelin, a tired Mathias ran 5:11 on a wet and slow track in the 1,500 meters to secure victory and become the youngest man ever to win a track and field gold medal, a record that still stands today. He finished with 7,139 points to capture the gold medal, while Ignace Heinrich of France was second with 6,974 points.

DEFENDING HIS TITLE

Mathias was the first athlete to successfully defend an Olympic decathlon title at the 1952 Games in Helsinki, Finland, where he also set Olympic and world records with his spectacular 7,887-point performance.

EYES OF THE WORLD
THE DEAD HELPS TEAM WIN BRONZE

Barcelona 1992: Basketball

While the Dream Team with Michael Jordan, Magic Johnson, and company were throttling the field on their way to a gold medal in men's basketball at the 1992 Summer Olympics—walloping Croatia by 32 points in the final—there was a tightly contested bronze medal game that oozed intrigue, was draped in historical significance, and featured colorful tie-dyed shirts, courtesy of the legendary rock band the Grateful Dead.

This was the first Summer Olympics that Lithuania was competing on its own, instead of being part of the Unified Team at the Olympics, which was the name for the sports team of the former Soviet Union. However, Lithuania's basketball team was financially strapped and in danger of not being able to compete. The Grateful Dead learned of Lithuania's plight and stepped up: they sent a large check and a box of tie-dyed T-shirts in Lithuania's national colors of red, yellow, and green with an image of a skeleton dunking a basketball.

The Lithuanian team featured Sarunas Marciulionis

STEPPING OUT FROM BEHIND THE IRON CURTAIN

Following the breakup of the Soviet Union in 1991, Lithuania was one of three ex-Soviet republics, along with Estonia and Latvia, that chose to compete individually instead of being part of the Unified Team at the 1992 Summer Games. Lithuania had been under communist rule of the Soviet Union since near the end of World War II.

and Arvydas Sabonis, two super-talented players who had successful NBA careers and were key pieces of the Soviet Union team that won the gold medal at the 1988 Olympics. Now, playing against their former teammates on the Unified Team, they were unstoppable. Marciulionis scored a game-high 29 points while Sabonis scored 27 points to lead Lithuania to an 82–78 win.

Lithuania wore their tie-dyed shirts on the medal stand while receiving their bronze medals.

WAITING 9 YEARS TO PLAY

Sabonis was a first-round draft pick of the Portland Trailblazers in 1986 but he didn't play his first game in the NBA until 1995 because Soviet officials refused to let him go to the United States.

LIKE A BUTTERFLY
THE GREATEST SHINES AGAIN

Atlanta 1996: Opening Ceremonies

The opening ceremonies of the 1996 Olympic Games in Atlanta featured the beautiful music of the Atlanta Symphony Orchestra, the legendary voices of Celine Dion and Gladys Knight, and the man who is widely considered the greatest boxer of all time, Muhammad Ali, lighting the Olympic flame while a worldwide audience watched in awe.

American swimming great Janet Evans, winner of four gold medals, ran up the ramp to the top of the stadium with a flaming torch in her right hand. Ali, the former three-time heavyweight boxing champion of the world, met her there. She touched her torch to his, and the great champion and humanitarian raised the torch above his head as the entire stadium of spectators and athletes embraced his presence. Then aged 54 and ravaged by Parkinson's disease, Ali gamely turned and lit a device that then slid along a wire to ignite the cauldron to signal the start of the Olympics.

In the lead up to the opening ceremonies, it was kept top secret that Ali would be lighting the flame. A week away from the big night, a rehearsal was held in the middle of the night, and until the day of the ceremonies Ali was hidden away in a private apartment.

Winner of the gold medal in the light heavyweight division at the 1960 Summer Olympics in Rome, Ali's appearance in Atlanta remains arguably the greatest moment in the history of Olympic opening ceremonies—which is only fitting for "The Greatest."

> "An honor. Mankind coming together. Martin Luther King's home. Muslims seeing me with the torch."
>
> – Muhammad Ali

In one of the greatest moments ever seen at an opening ceremony for the Summer Olympics, Muhammad Ali lights the flame to signal the start of The Games in Atlanta in 1996.

DREAM COMES TRUE
WIN FULFILLS DEATHBED PROMISE

2008 Beijing: Weightlifting

When Olympians step onto the podium to receive their medals, it is often an emotionally charged moment, the result of long and hard years of training and making huge sacrifices in the pursuit of being the best in the world. For German weightlifter Matthias Steiner, who won a gold medal in the super heavyweight weightlifting class in Beijing in 2008, his trip to the podium involved tears of happiness as well as heartbreak.

In June 2007, the weightlifter's 22-year-old wife Susann died of injuries sustained after her compact car was hit head-on by an SUV being driven on the wrong side of the road. While she lay in the hospital, Steiner made a bedside promise to her that he would keep their Olympic gold medal dream. Doing so required him to call upon every morsel of strength he could find.

In the clean and jerk, Steiner failed on his first attempt at 246 kilograms (542.33 pounds). He then lifted 248 kilograms on his next attempt, but when Russia's Evgeny Chigishev succeeded at 250 kilograms (551.15 pounds), Steiner had to make an attempt at 258 kilograms (568.79 pounds), the heaviest weight he had ever tried to lift. When he was finally able to get the weight above his head and saw the judge's signal that it was a good lift, Steiner dropped the weight and jumped up and down in pure joy. When he was presented his gold medal Steiner proudly displayed a photo of his wife, marking one of the most beautiful moments in Olympic medal ceremony history.

"She is always with me. In the hours before the competition she's there."
– Matthias Steiner

German weightlifter Matthias Steiner fulfilled a deathbed promise to his wife by winning a gold medal at the 2008 Beijing Olympics with this lift of 258 kilograms in the clean and jerk.

FIRST FOR FEMALES
WOMEN ALLOWED TO COMPETE

Paris 1900: Multiple Events

As the Summer Olympic Games have evolved through the decades there have been many signature moments that have helped mold and define what this must-see global spectacle is all about. One of the most important of those took place in 1900 when women were allowed to compete for the first time when the Olympics were held in Paris in conjunction with the World's Fair. During the ancient Olympics, women did not participate. Pierre de Coubertin, the founder of the International Olympic Committee who organized the 1896 Games in Athens, was against women competing.

Tennis and golf were the only events held just for women in Paris, while they also competed against the men in several other events that included croquet, rowing, sailing, archery, and equestrian. Nearly 1,000 athletes from 24 countries participated, dozens of whom were women.

There were some terrific female athletes competing in Paris, including Swiss sailor and first-ever female gold medalist Helen de Pourtales and Britain's Charlotte Cooper, one of the best tennis players of her era. When Cooper arrived in Paris, she had already won three Wimbledon titles. Lawn tennis had two Olympic events—singles and mixed doubles. She won both, in

GOLDEN GOLFING GIRL

Margaret Abbott and her mom Mary arrived in Paris in 1899 for the World's Fair. Both were good golfers, so when they learned there was an international golf tournament taking place they entered. Margaret's round of 47 on the nine-hole course was the best in the 19-player field, making her the first American woman to win an Olympic event. Her mom was seventh.

the process becoming the first individual female Olympic champion.

Croquet was in the Olympic line-up for the first and only time. The field of 10 competitors featured three French women—Marie Ohnier, Jeanne Filleul-Brohy, and a woman listed only as Mrs. Després.

CONFUSING SET-UP

Organizers conducted the Olympics in conjunction with the World's Fair and they spread the competitions out over a five-month period. It was such an unusual format that many athletes didn't even know they were competing in the Olympics.

GAME CHANGING EVENTS

MELBOURNE, AUSTRALIA

Seven countries boycotted these games, including the Netherlands, Switzerland, and Spain. These three were protesting Soviet military action in Hungary, a conflict that played out in competition. The IOC allowed the Soviets to compete, and in water polo they played Hungary in a semifinal match that turned violent. "Blood in the Water" screamed the headlines. Hungary won and went on to claim gold.

LONDON, UK

After six years of World War II, the world looked to war-ravaged London to pull off the first Olympics since 1936 (Germany and Japan were banned). It was not easy. These were dubbed the Austerity Games in a London that was broke. No new stadiums were built, and food was rationed, but the Games themselves were a huge success.

MUNICH, GERMANY

The 1972 Munich Games were marred attack on the Olympic Village. Palest terrorists killed two Israeli athletes and nine others hostage. The drama played on live television around the worl botched rescue attempt 20 hours late all nine Israeli hostages and five of terrorists dead.

POLITICS... CRISIS... SOCIAL CHANGE

FOR USE BY WHITE PERSONS

THESE PUBLIC PREMISES AND THE AMENITIES
THEREOF HAVE BEEN RESERVED FOR THE
EXCLUSIVE USE OF WHITE PERSONS.

By Order   Provincial Secretary

VIR GEBRUIK DEUR BLANKES

HIERDIE OPENBARE PERSEEL EN DIE GERIEWE
DAARVAN IS VIR DIE UITSLUITLIKE GEBRUIK
VAN BLANKES AANGEWYS.

Op Las   Provinsiale Sekretaris

MOSCOW, USSR

In December of 1979, Soviet troops attacked the Afghan capital of Kabul, executed president Hafizullah Amin and made Babrak Karmal, who was a Soviet supporter, the new leader. This kicked off what would become a 10-year occupation. The United States led the idea of boycotting the Games if the Soviets did not withdraw, and ultimately more than 60 countries decided not to send athletes to Moscow.

MONTREAL, CANADA

nty-two African nations boycotted 1976 Montreal Games at the last ute when the IOC allowed New and to participate after having sent ugby team to play in South Africa. South African government was subject of international scorn and ctions due to its policy of racial egation called apartheid.

RIO DE JANEIRO, BRAZIL

The IOC allowed 10 athletes without a country to participate under the Olympic flag. Amidst a worldwide refugee crisis, the IOC funded the training for the selected athletes. Examples of what they had survived include the Syrian Civil War and tribal genocide in the Democratic Republic of the Congo.

RESEARCH PROJECTS

Major moments on the world stage have impacted the Olympics through the years. The following Research Projects will bring a deeper perspective to these moments and the events that shaped them.

1. The U.S.-led boycott of the 1980 Games in Moscow was followed by the Soviet-led boycott of the 1984 Los Angeles Games. Writing from the point of view of the leader of each country, write a 200-word op-ed article for each outlining the reasons why boycotting the games was justified.

2. South Africa is a country with a population that is more than 80 percent black and less than 10 percent white. From 1948 to 1991, it was run under a system of institutionalized segregation of the races known as apartheid. This system discriminated against the majority black population, making it illegal for people of different races to live in the same area, to marry, or to use the same beaches, buses, schools or hospitals, among many other things. Research the international sporting boycott that arose due to apartheid, and how South Africa would eventually be banned from the Olympics beginning with the 1964 Tokyo Games.

3. Research the events that took place prior to, at, and after the 1936 Berlin Olympics as they applied to American sprinter Jesse Owens, the German Nazi party, and the life Owens returned to after those Games. Focus on the decision to attend the Games, what Owens was told to expect versus want happened in Berlin, and how Owens was treated when he returned home.

4. At the 1968 Games in Mexico City, 200-meter medalists Tommie Smith and John Carlos of the USA made a statement by delivering a Black Power salute as they stood on the medal podium. Research the incident to find out what the gesture meant, why they did it, and what the reaction was at the time. Also include a perspective on how the action is viewed today.

5. Memories of the best performances from the 100-year centennial of the Olympics in Atlanta in 1996 cannot block out the horror of a bombing that left two people dead and more than 100 injured. Research what happened, including where the attack took place, who was initially held responsible and how the investigation unfolded. Present your findings in the form of three distinct news articles.

OLYMPIC GLOSSARY OF KEY TERMS

archery—the sport of shooting arrows with a bow.

banned—to prohibit, especially by legal means.

compete—to strive consciously or unconsciously for an objective (such as position, profit, or a prize).

decathlon—an athletic contest consisting of ten different track and field events.

doping—the use of a substance (such as an anabolic steroid or erythropoietin) or technique (such as blood doping) to illegally improve athletic performance.

equestrian—of, relating to, or featuring horseback riding.

heat—one of several preliminary contests held to eliminate less competent contenders.

host city—the city that is selected to be the primary location for Olympic ceremonies and events.

hurdle—a light barrier that competitors must leap over in races.

medal—a piece of metal often resembling a coin and having a stamped design that is issued to commemorate a person or event or awarded for excellence or achievement; may also mean to win a medal.

nationality—a legal relationship involving allegiance on the part of an individual and usually protection on the part of the state.

opponent—a contestant that you are matched against.

participant—a person who takes part in something.

preliminary—a minor match preceding the main event.

pommel horse—a gymnastics apparatus for swinging and balancing feats that consists of a padded rectangular or cylindrical form with two handgrips called pommels on the top and that is supported in a horizontal position above the floor.

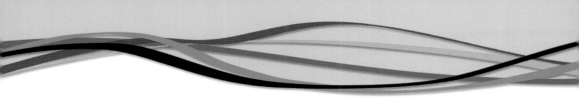

qualify—meet the required standard.

referee—the official in a sport who is expected to ensure fair play.

repechage—a race (especially in rowing) in which runners-up in the eliminating heats compete for a place in the final race.

spectator—one who looks on or watches.

sportsmanship—fairness, honesty, and courtesy in following the rules of a game.

stamina—enduring strength and energy.

standings—an ordered listing of scores or results showing the relative positions of competitors (individuals or teams) in an event.

substitute—a player or competitor that takes the place of another.

torch—a cylindrical or cone-shaped object in which the Olympic flame is ceremonially carried.

vault—to execute a leap using the hands or a pole.

venue—the place where any event or action is held.

victory—a successful ending of a struggle or contest; a win.

EDUCATIONAL VIDEO LINKS

Bolt Smashes Two World Records: http://x-qr.net/1J5B
Freeman Delivers for Her People: http://x-qr.net/1K6r
Johnson Sets 200 Meters Record: http://x-qr.net/1Kq7
Phelps Wins Eight Gold Medals: http://x-qr.net/1KvA
Rudisha is Fastest of The Fast: http://x-qr.net/1Jqz
Rulon Gardner Wins Gold: http://x-qr.net/1LJH
Runner Finishes with Dad's Help: http://x-qr.net/1L3F
Sailor Pulls Two Men from Sea: http://x-qr.net/1LCb
Soviet Strongman Sets Record: http://x-qr.net/1LpJ
Sprinters Protest on the Podium: http://x-qr.net/1JQy
The Greatest Shines Again: http://x-qr.net/1JXp
Win Fulfills Deathbed Promise: http://x-qr.net/1LuL

FURTHER READING

Boykoff, Jules. *Power Games: A Political History of the Olympics.* New York: Verso, 2016.

Goldblatt, David. *The Games: A Global History of the Olympics*. New York: W. W. Norton & Company, 2018.

Olympic Museum. *The Treasures of the Olympic Games: An Interactive History of the Olympic Games.* London: Carlton Books, 2016.

Phelps, Michael, and Brian Cazeneuve. *Beneath the Surface: My Story*. Champaign: Sports Publishing, 2016.

River, Charles, ed. *The Ancient Olympic Games: The History and Legacy of Ancient Greece's Most Famous Sports Event*. Brookfield: Charles River Publishing, 2016.

INTERNET RESOURCES

www.olympic.org/
The official website of the IOC. The site features the latest news and information regarding the Olympics, an archive of results and photos from past Olympic Games, and information on the IOC and its members.

www.teamusa.org/
The official website of the United States Olympic & Paralympic Committee. Included on this site are profiles of Team USA athletes and the latest news and results from competitions involving U.S. athletes worldwide. Plus, there is a real-time clock counting down to the start of the 2020 Summer Olympics in Tokyo.

www.nbcolympics.com/
The website of NBC Sports, which is covering the 2020 Summer Olympics. A breakdown of all the events that will be contested in Tokyo are included, along with the latest Olympic news from around the world.

www.olympicchannel.com/en/
The official website of the Olympic Channel. The site features profiles of past and present Olympians, access to original programming, and the latest news and information regarding the Olympics.

www.espn.com/olympics/
This web page is ESPN's coverage of everything related to the Olympics, including all the latest news and information regarding Olympic athletes from around the world.

INDEX

PHOTO CREDITS

Shutterstock.com: Eastimages: 7, kovop58: 9, Pete Niesen: 18, Mitch Gunn: 42, Leonard Zhukovsky: 46, Nature Diver: 54, Leonard Zhukovsky: 73

Alamy Stock Photos: PA Images: 12, 30, 50, INTERFOTO: 28

Wikimedia Commons: UPI: 14, Unknown author: 16, 38, 70 Public domain: 20, 32, Albert Meyer: 24, Associated Press: 40, Unknown (Asahi Shinbun)/Public domain: 44, Paul Rowlett from Sheffield, UK: 48, Parliament Speakers Limited: 52, UPI: 56, Angelo Cozzi (Mondadori Publishers)/Public domain: 58, McSmit: 60, Anefo: 62, National Media Museum from UK: 72, Thaler Tamas: 72, High Contrast: 72, Dewet: 73, NFYFLY: 73

Dreamstime.com: Jerry Coli: 22, 26, 34, Sean Pavone: 66

Flickr: Findingmuse: 36, stannate: 64, Dacoucou: 68

All background images provided by Shutterstock and Dreamstime

AUTHOR BIOGRAPHY

GREG BACH is the author of 10 books, including titles on sports and coaching. Growing up in Swartz Creek, Michigan, he has been a lifelong fan of the Detroit Tigers and has fond memories of attending games with his family at the old Tiger Stadium. He is a proud graduate of Michigan State University and resides in West Palm Beach, Florida.